Praise for *My Secret Life with Chris Noth*

Iris N. Schwartz's latest book, *My Secret Life with Chris Noth: And Other Stories* (Poets Wear Prada), is a small collection of flash fiction that a reader can read in one sitting because it simply can't be put down.

— **NILES REDDICK**, *MIDWEST BOOK REVIEW*

Only from the creative world of an Iris N. Schwartz story would the contents of a boyfriend's refrigerator be the cause for a change in their relationship — or a Jewish girl coming-of-age story have her falling for the first blond guy she's ever met. And then there's the music that plays a part throughout much of her work as do physical limitations and dreams. Oh, the dreams! Don't ask. Read. You'll end up like me — a fan. A fan who wants to be let in on more of Ms. Schwartz's world.

— **PAUL BECKMAN**, AUTHOR OF *PEEK*

In *My Secret Life with Chris Noth*, Iris N. Schwartz delivers nine perfect tales — each one delicately embroidered with the clearest of details, populated by characters so real and human you'll think you know them. Her prose has a light touch but an effect that lingers long after the page. Please treat yourself to this collection.

— **JONATHAN CARDEW**, FICTION EDITOR, *CONNOTATION PRESS*

Iris N. Schwartz employs straightforward, clean writing with attitude to tell her stories of family, romance, and coming of age.

— GAY DEGANI, AUTHOR OF *WHAT CAME BEFORE*

These nine stories are beautifully written; sometimes funny, sometimes sad, and many times both together. The characters feel real. Flawed and imperfect and often trapped, here are the ways they try to find freedom. Through love, through fiction, through "The Light Show," through Chris Noth! Thanks to Iris N. Schwartz, we can escape alongside them.

— CHRISTOPHER JAMES, FOUNDING EDITOR, *JELLYFISH REVIEW*

You might be familiar with the characters in this collection. One might be that girl you'd known as a child, another that young woman you'd met on a date. They could be Everyperson; they could be you or me. But the stories go much deeper than that. Iris N. Schwartz uses precise, spiky prose to take us on short journeys across psychic landscapes. We easily experience the sensations and emotions of her characters. And as in many journeys, the destination often is unexpected. It is a place of recognition, yet it can seem foreign. When you get there, you've come to know a little bit more about the people around you — and about yourself.

— THADDEUS RUTKOWSKI, AUTHOR OF *GUESS AND CHECK*

Iris N. Schwartz has written a book that, in turn, caused me to feel delight, uneasiness, terror, sadness, chills and, finally, returned me to delight. Her characters, often children, reach out to us and haunt us with their visions, troubles and fantasies — you want to jump into the stories and take them in your arms. I will remember these stories for a long time and look forward to reading more of this wonderful author's work.

— **SIAN BARBARA ALLEN, RETIRED TV AND FILM STAR**

Nine wonderful stories by Iris N. Schwartz, stories so real, so human, stories that will stay with you long after reading.

— **DIGBY BEAUMONT, FLASH FICTION WRITER, HOVE, ENGLAND**

Love drives every sentence and nuance in these short tight flash fictions from the pen of Iris N. Schwartz. In a clean economic prose style, she crooks a finger and we follow her down into dank basements for phone trysts, into bowling alleys where monarch butterflies flit above the head of a modern blond Adonis, or into her dreams where Chris Noth appears, from time to time, to enchant. And, there is more. Schwartz allows us all a little dream-time, here. But she knows where she's headed and her writer feet are firmly planted. A very highly recommended collection.

— **SUSAN TEPPER, AUTHOR OF *WHAT DRIVES MEN***

These flashes are warm, vivid, and complete. The individual humanity really shines, and you have to love the surprises that manage to occur in such short spaces. Very nice.

— DAVID S. ATKINSON, AUTHOR OF *ROSES ARE RED, VIOLETS ARE STEALING LOOSE CHANGE FROM MY POCKETS WHILE I SLEEP*

shame

Also by Iris N. Schwartz

My Secret Life with Chris Noth: And Other Stories, Hoboken, NJ: Poets Wear Prada, 2017

Awakened: Poetry by Madeline Artenberg / Poetry by Iris N. Schwartz, with Madeline Artenberg, New York, NY: Rogue Scholars Press, 2006

s h a m e

and other stories

IRIS N. SCHWARTZ

POETS WEAR PRADA • Hoboken, New Jersey

SHAME

Poets Wear Prada
533 Bloomfield Street, Second Floor
Hoboken, New Jersey 07030
http://pwpbooks.blogspot.com

First North American Publication 2019
First Mass Market Paperback Edition 2019

Grateful acknowledgment is made to the following publications where some of these stories originally appeared:

Anti-Heroin Chic, Blink-Ink, The Drabble, Five:2:One, Foxglove Journal, Friday Flash Fiction, Jellyfish Review, The Round Up Zine, and *Spelk*

ISBN-13: 978-1-946116-01-7 ISBN-10: 1-946116-01-7

Library of Congress Control Number: 2018953771

Printed in the U.S.A.

Front Cover Image: Meredith Marsone, *Slave*, 2015, oil on canvas, 40" x 60", private collection

Author Photo: Roxanne Hoffman

For David B., Lydia B., and Sam P.,
with love

Table of Contents

shame

AT LIBERTY

B elle never should have married a man who didn't know how to kiss. Benjy's sloppy, aimless probing of her mouth felt as erotic as a session in a dentist's chair.

He was dyslexic and fumbled for words. She often imagined casting a fishing rod into Benjy's throat to find and reel in synonyms superior to the words he chose.

The man possessed a notably small vocabulary, relying on "nice" and, when elated, "very nice." If she heard one more "very nice dress" or "nice movie we saw last night," she would retch. Heavy-duty retching, maybe even projectile.

Why had Belle, a Columbia University MFA student and avid reader, married a man who hadn't finished high school and who read, at the most, a book a year? At the time of her wedding she was 32, ached for children, thought 38-year-old Benjy a good man, and talked herself into loving him.

Soon after they separated, Belle stuffed her four-year-old wedding gown into a no-name trash bag, carted it down to her apartment building's basement, and pressed it into the only empty garbage can. That night she dreamed she strolled to a nearby vacant lot. There she saw a familiar lace sleeve and dirt-tinged train. Her wedding dress!

As she leaned in closer, she observed maybe thirty gowns strewn over the lot, each looking dingy and forlorn. Belle cried out, "I must rescue you!" and awakened to a tug in her throat, a desire to sob that she would not give in to.

She returned to sleep, shaken. In her next dream a handsomely aged woman told Belle to retrieve the gown and bury it. The old woman would tell her no more; Belle, she offered, must discover the rest for herself.

Belle reawakened, curiously calm and expectant. She showered, dressed, decided to take a walk before work. Before she made her way to the subway, Belle noticed the lot was no longer vacant. She took in rich coffee-colored soil; lush jade-green vegetation; fragrant, brilliantly hued blossoms. When had all this happened?

Emerging from the soil, between every shrub and flowerbed, were sleeves, hems, bodices. A sign, plunged into the dirt, read:

PLEASE DO NOT DISTURB WEDDING ATTIRE
FLOWERS OR VEGETABLES
WORN WEDDING GOWNS ENRICH AND NURTURE
PLEASE ALLOW OUR GARDEN TO GROW

Belle cried happily. Her gown had found a home — "a very nice" home.

EVER AFTER

Paula knew her relationship with Vic would improve after they married. How could it not? She was in love.

The plump but petite thirty-two-year-old redhead, Paula Baumgarten, met the famous thirty-seven-year-old restaurateur at cooking school. A burly, tall, silver-haired Vic Pinkler popped into Classic Desserts to show the class how to make banana cream pie, his trademark dessert, staple of his chain — and one of Paula's specialties. After sampling her rendition, which she fed to him on a fork, Vic invited Paula to talk food over dinner.

They started dating and soon uncovered a second mutual passion. Cinema. Paula adored old films, especially romantic comedies like *His Gal Friday* and *The Philadelphia Story*; Vic amassed vintage black-and-white movies, primarily 1950s film noir classics like *Kiss Me Deadly* and *D.O.A.* He looked forward to building floor-to-ceiling walnut media cabinets for their joint DVD film collection and to alphabetizing titles within genre. She looked forward to teaching Vic the finer points of lovemaking and to spending time with him in the kitchen.

Once the couple married, while Vic continued to

acquire DVDs and restaurants, Paula doted on rolling pins, hamburger presses, and other humble kitchen collectibles. She had cooked and baked with these items and once considered a career in catering. Now her kitchen tools were shelved behind the shiny glass doors of her husband's handiwork.

Evenings Vic liked to stay home, lay his hands on the jewel cases of DVDs and on the body of his bride. Ever since their country club wedding in Woodmere, Long Island, Vic made it his business to provide for Mrs. Pinkler's every pleasure.

He brought in chefs from his restaurants to prepare specialties for her: pork cheeks and quinoa with kale-leek compote one night; veal medallions with trumpet mushrooms and elephant-garlic puree the next.

Vic imagined holding a plate to his wife's face to watch her lick it clean. He called her his poodle. Eight months after their wedding, she was thirty pounds overweight — but that made her even more bountiful to him. He was more than twenty pounds heavier than when they met.

After each evening repast, after the help cleared the dining room table, Paula's personal assistant, Aurora, laid out a peignoir and negligee but only after drawing a bath. Vic permitted his wife to bathe herself but always insisted on massaging her with floral-scented cream afterward. He wanted her soft and aromatic for their bedchambers.

No one mentioned the violet bruises that dotted Paula's pink body after Vic rubbed her down.

Paula's heart no longer fluttered when Vic kissed her. Instead, her stomach churned. He was boorish, mashed his lips onto hers, allowed spittle to collect in the corners of his mouth. He did not caress or blow on her skin as he had early on. He rubbed her as if eradicating stains.

Early in their marriage, Paula believed she could teach Vic to make love to her in ways she preferred. Any touch that even hinted at finesse was rewarded with an "ooh" or "yes." But he never caught on and didn't take to special requests. Eventually, Paula faked orgasms — as soon and as loudly as possible — during each encounter. Anything to put an end to his dull manhandling. She often wondered if Vic even noticed.

VIC PINKLER FELT anxious about his wife traveling on her own anywhere, within Long Island or — God forbid! — to Manhattan, so he provided her with a driver for her "jaunts." Paula Pinkler had always previously traveled by herself to cooking school or to estate sales to hunt for that new piece of depression glass or one-of-a-kind egg plate, but it was easier to slide onto the back seat of the Lincoln and let Errol drive. And the couple would no longer have to discuss her safety. Did Errol report on her whereabouts? Paula chose not to think about that possibility.

IT WAS UNSEASONABLY steamy that Tuesday in May when Paula asked Errol to bring the car around. She generally wore long sleeves but that day sported a sleeveless shell under a linen three-quarter-sleeve jacket. She would be comfortable but maintain coverage. Aurora murmured approval.

Paula had seen an advertisement for a nearby estate sale. Photos of vintage rooster canister sets and farm-motif dinnerware had riveted her attention. She realized she hadn't been to a sale or auction for months.

She recalled rolling dough for a lattice-top peach pie — arms strengthening with each back-and-forth motion, mouth blowing upwards to cool sweaty bangs — then tasting Freestone peach juice on her fingertips.

She saw Errol nodding at her in the rear-view mirror. She cleared her throat, smoothed her lips. He had caught her smiling.

✍

UPON INSPECTING the items for sale, Paula felt disappointment — like a peach pit — lodged in her throat. Nothing looked as good as what she already owned. The place was stuffy. She felt hemmed in. Paula pushed up her sleeves, fanned her face with one hand.

Someone grabbed her shoulder. Strong grip, thin fingers. She tried to pull away without looking at the intruder. Fingers snapped before Paula's face. She heard a familiar voice ask: "Paula, is that you?"

Paula recognized her Basic Mediterranean Cuisine classmate Gloria LaSalle. The woman's eyes were darting from Paula's forearms to Paula's face. Then the woman stepped back and gazed at Paula from head to toe.

Why, thought Paula, did she leave the house today? She considered pretending not to recognize Gloria. Maybe even feign illness. Paula's life felt like a bad movie: disagreeable characters, questionable script.

Two arms pulled her away from chattering buyers and gleaming wares toward an empty hallway. Paula found herself seated on a tufted chair, holding a handkerchief offered by Gloria, blotting endless tears and disobedient mascara.

Her former classmate pointed at the bruises on Paula's wrists and forearms. Gloria's mouth was moving fast: "Who's doing this to you? Why do you put up with it?"

⸎

GLORIA LASALLE ENLISTED the help of Errol. That same day, despite Aurora's protests, Errol packed up Paula's belongings — most of her clothes, shoes, and handbags; all of her kitchen collectibles and favorite DVDs — to take to Gloria's house in Elmont. At Paula's request, Errol left the jewelry boxes untouched.

That evening, when Vic Pinkler arrived home, he found

several cabinet shelves and curio cases empty. The flat-screen TVs, oil paintings, sound system, bedroom safe, and jewelry boxes were untouched. He didn't notice the paucity of clothes in Paula's closet. He thought they had been robbed — by a finicky, eccentric thief. Vic phoned the police.

Errol and Aurora called contacts to secure new jobs.

Gloria LaSalle pressured Paula to stay in Elmont.

Paula felt extremely fortunate to have run into Gloria. Paula asked Gloria for help finding an apartment. Gloria agreed and also offered to help Paula locate a catering job. To show her gratitude, Paula Baumgarten promised herself she would start eating less the very next day.

THE NEW MATH

N inth-grade math: effortless? Addition, subtraction, multiplication, division: common sense. English, history, social studies, science: a breeze. Four breezes.

Algebra: tangle of numbers, letters, punctuation. Chalk hieroglyphs commandeering blackboard. Trap set not with cheddar but equations. Waste of Carly's (otherwise) nimble mind.

Unless Carly guilted her parents into hiring tutors? Cheated? She could write on her palms, her sneaker soles, slips of paper folded accordion-like and hidden up her sleeves. Stole? Copies of previous tests. Maybe pop classmate Shelly on the head, grab her notes while she lies unconscious.

Carly required A's. Had a reputation. Needed Valedictorian status, multiple Harvard degrees. By any computation necessary.

YELLOW

L illian has lost three blonde cousins at the Dobroville State Fair. Everyone there is yellow haired except her and Corn Dog USA's Niblette Johnson — both brunette. At Guess Your Weight a tow-haired oldster turns and points, shouting: "New York!" Convinced he means Jew, Lillian backs away. One cousin strawberry, another dirty, the third platinum. Finding them should be a cinch, she tells herself.

SHAME

Hudson View Rehabilitation, New York City. A Monday afternoon in February 2017.

From an intercom inside a patient's room: Static. Then: "Didn't you just have a diaper change?"

Lying in a hospital bed, Joseph Fein, a thirty-eight-year-old accountant, thrust his throbbing right arm toward the edge of the mattress. The tissue box was a thumb's length away. "Yes, I just had a diaper change."

Silence from the intercom.

"I'm not happy wearing diapers. I hope to return to a life of continence ASAP," he continued, still struggling to reach the tissue box.

Outside the patient's room, seated at the nurses' station, Nurse Giselle Williams bristled. She had offended the man. What had she been thinking? Too many back-to-back shifts, she concluded. She needed some strong coffee. She checked the clock radio by the monitors; it was almost break time.

∽

FOOTSTEPS. The door to his tiny room opened. Joseph was lying flat on his back, swathed in bedclothes, wearing only a tie-back gown and adult briefs. He studied the forty-something woman as she took charge of the space. Shoulder-length braids, imperious cheekbones, curves contained by her sex-negating uniform. (In other circumstances, maybe he would have sidled up, offered a beer. Maybe not. She was too beautiful.)

Giselle carried in a pink plastic bucket containing incontinence supplies — cleaning cloths, protective cream, disposable chucks, and two fresh adult briefs — which she placed on the rolling tray table by his bed. After adjusting the hospital bed and helping him out of his bedclothes, she started to unfasten his diaper: left tab, then right.

Joseph caught her nostrils flaring at the earthy aroma as she pulled away the front of his diaper.

"Can you roll over on your side?" she asked.

He groaned as she gently rolled him to face away so she could properly remove the soiled diaper from between his legs. He could not see the tears brimming in her eyes as she disposed of the fetid brief wrapped neatly inside the old chuck. Or see her smile of relief as she changed gloves before placing two layers of fresh chucks beside him.

She deftly scrubbed his rectum and cheeks, inner thighs, pubic area, testicles, and penis before removing the top chuck and tossing it in the trash. She switched gloves again, applied him with the protective cream, then positioned and repositioned the new diaper, finally fastening its right tab.

"Okay, you can face me now." She returned him to supine position as he sighed with relief to be lying, less uncomfortably, on his back.

Grateful, he watched her finish fastening the fourth diaper of his adult life.

Giselle retrieved the box of tissues, which had fallen to the floor, placing it within Joseph's reach on the bed.

"Thank you, Nurse . . . " said Joseph, wishing he'd asked her name. The closing door sliced through his thoughts. Cleansed, Joseph rearranged his private parts within the diaper.

∽

BREAK TIME. Time for Giselle to secure that cup of coffee.

NICKLED-AND-DIMED

Brooklyn, New York — 1967

I nterrupting episode 22 of "Love on a Rooftop" — as a knock on the door halted the newlyweds Dave and Julie Willis's kiss — Lenore, eight, announced she had swallowed a nickel. Her voice was low; her words measured.

Her older sister, Imogene, eleven, rushed over. "Are you sure?"

Lenore nodded.

Imogene paced the living room, muttering: "How could this happen?" Regarding her younger sister, seated on the sofa, attentively watching Judy Carne, Imogene probed again: "Are you sure?"

A champagne supper was being wheeled into the newlyweds' hotel room. Violins were playing.

Lenore smiled, slightly.

"Why? On the one night Dad and Mother go out!"

⁓

IMOGENE WAS SPEAKING with an emergency operator. She was answering questions: "no, I don't know how it happened" and "yes, she's breathing fine."

Imogene hung up, shut off the TV, glared at Lenore: "You better not be making this up!"

"I'm not."

"Because if you are —"

The rear doorbell rang. Two lanky young men in uniform were at the back door. "Is this the household with the coin swallower?"

Lenore prayed the officers wouldn't spot the mold on the mezuzah as her older sister invited the policemen into the family's eat-in kitchen.

Officer Blond sat down at the unsteady kitchen table. Officer Brunet wandered into the living room, stopping to examine the family's antique glass-door bookcase.

"Can I get you coffee?" Imogene asked, her eyes on Brunet, who appeared to be transfixed by the bookcase. "Gum?" she offered, wondering if he was planning to nest.

Blond: "No, we're fine."

Officer Brunet re-entered the kitchen. He and Blond questioned Lenore about how she'd come to swallow the coin, a Buffalo nickel she had "collected" and was "examining in the dark." She: "Didn't want to bother my sister by turning on a light." But when the eight-year-old held the nickel high to catch the dwindling sunlight from the window, Lenore recounted, the coin tumbled from an unsteady hand into her startled mouth.

Blond: "Any trouble breathing since the incident?"

"No," Lenore said, spotting a humongous water bug under the table, inching toward Blond. She wondered if he had noticed.

Brunet asked the older sister about their parents' whereabouts.

"Oh, God, they're at a PTA meeting. They're going out for dinner afterward. They haven't been out in years!"

Brunet: "Well, we need a family member over eighteen to tell us whether she'll stay here or go to the hospital."

Lenore gulped. She hadn't been to a hospital since her tonsillectomy. And then she hadn't gotten the ice cream she'd been promised. Just some runny red gelatin. No, she told herself, she wouldn't go! She stomped, aimed for the water bug as it sped away.

Imogene decided their parents should be called back home.

⸺ ⸱⸱⸱ ⸺

DAD GRUMBLED. This was the first time in three years they had gone out, only to be rushed back home — early! Mother had on makeup like Judy Carne. The sisters knew not to look her in the eye: her eyes made massive by mascara; theirs not.

Blond told Dad and Mother that Lenore could get her stomach pumped in the hospital or wait a few days at home for the collectible coin, encouraged by fibrous food and lots of water, to pass.

Brunet admired the glass-door bookcase aloud; he asked if it was available for sale. Dad and Mother, simultaneously and vigorously, shook their heads no.

———❧———

NATURE WAS ALLOWED to take its course; Lenore was spared a trip to the hospital.

Dad and Mother didn't yell or spank. Mostly Dad grunted; Mother favored silence.

Two days later a dusky Buffalo nickel, accompanied by a handwritten sign, was taped to the door leading to the basement. Dad's joke would remain on that door for a year for all who came to see.

Imogene and Lenore had dreams involving Officers Blond and Brunet till early spring.

Every Thursday night, the family watched "Love on a Rooftop" until its final episode that April. Dad and Mother agreed, like Dave and Julie, their perfect place was home.

GIFTS FROM GOD

Nathania "Niblette" Johnson believes the surname *Niblett* once described people — Jews or Africans — with sizable aquiline noses. Her late father, Nathan "Niblett," appropriated the noble old name for his own fine, broad ebony nose and for the cayenne-peppered, whole kernel and cornmeal batter used for his all-natural, deep-fried hot dogs. Her given name like his means "gift from God." The crunchy, savory treasures Nathania serves at Corn Dog USA are also gifts from God. Just ask her customers.

FUR

Two nights ago, after plumping up her pillow but before switching off her bedside table lamp, Dahlia noticed a hamster-size hologram of a cat, nestled beside her, on the bed. The hologram cat, a milky calico, was curled up upon the pillow, silently kneading it with a paw.

At first she was drawn in, awed by the minute details of its tiny features, but then Dahlia became frightened and looked away. When she dared to return her gaze to the pillow, the miniature feline had vanished.

Panic overcame the forty-five-year-old widow. How could there have been a hologram? Must have been a hallucination! Perhaps a side effect of her new sleep medication? That possibility did not improve her state of mind.

The following morning, in the pitch-black of two o'clock, Dahlia caught sight of a life-size kitty perched on top of the desk chair. As she scratched the creature behind the ears, the woman sighed with relief — and disappointment — that it felt more like cotton than cat. Dahlia was, in fact, scratching cotton T-shirts and pullovers.

Dahlia's first cat, an overweight silver tabby partial to

classical piano, had died at the age of thirteen after its kidneys shut down. Her second cat, a black-and-white tuxedo with the most delicate pink nose and the most intensely green eyes she'd ever seen, passed away at the age of seven after a neurological condition left it disposed to leaning to the left and foaming at the mouth.

Of course, Dahlia missed a Felis catus scampering about the house, hissing at birds. She hadn't known, however, how desperate her need was until she experienced the hallucinations.

People argue; cats purr — a soothing substitute for talk. Cats go about their secretive business in the back of a closet or under the bed, affording a person time to use social media, apply makeup, watch TV. Dogs, by contrast, are always up in your business, begging for love and play.

Cats calm you, lower your blood pressure. Humans? Often, the opposite. And cats never beg for affection. They know they deserve it. Good role models, cats.

Dahlia shook herself out of her reverie. She didn't want to go crazy from the lack of feline. Tomorrow she'd investigate rescues.

———⚬∞⚬———

THE DOORBELL RANG, repeatedly. Dahlia squinted at her alarm clock: six a.m.! Who could it be? The doorbell sounded again, followed by a series of scratches. Dahlia donned a robe, walked to the kitchen, and drew back the curtains. Across the street stood a coach with two horses! She did not see a footman.

Once again, the doorbell rang.

"Okay, okay!" The woman unlatched and slowly opened her front door.

A graying but handsome Maine Coon, standing erect at six feet and attired in a natty blue suit, was licking one of its huge paws. "Is Madam ready," it asked, "to go shopping for cats?"

Dahlia smiled. "Give me ten minutes, please. I'll need to get dressed and get my coat."

SPECIAL

He said he had a "special" place she could touch. A sensitive place. Kept turning to her, grinning, as he drove.

She didn't want to get into a car accident, or displease him, so she smiled back.

"Want to know where it is?"

She looked at his flannel-shirted chest, concentrated on the plaid pattern. Crimson Wallace. Thin lines of gold crisscrossed intersections of black and red.

His right hand grazed her cheek. "Do you?"

"Do I what?" She glanced down at his blue-jeaned thighs. Looked up: his hair was dark, curly — wild. Avoided his face.

"Want to see my sensitive place? Come on, give me your hand."

They were in the park now. Late afternoon. She was hungry. Dizzy. Too much sun. Gary — was that his name? — hadn't offered brunch, not even coffee.

He pulled over, turned off the engine. Placed her left hand on his thigh. "You were looking *here*, right?"

She didn't pull her hand away. Her eyes on his shirt,

she thought of her brother. It was summer. They were still just kids. Her brother had crossed his legs, the slit on his crimson plaid boxers had opened onto . . . something she shouldn't have seen.

Gary: "You weren't this quiet on the phone."

Dumb-ass, she thought. How could she be quiet on the phone and keep a conversation going?

He inched her hand up his thigh. "You're getting closer to my special place." He grinned again.

An original thinker — just like St. Thomas Aquinas or Charles Darwin! "I can figure out where it is," she said.

"Really?" Gary or Larry Dumb-ass brought her hand further up his molten thigh.

She shivered. Fingertips freezing.

"Let me show you." He tugged her hand up higher, so it practically cupped a testicle through the denim.

She removed her hand. Looked away. Heard him draw down his zipper. Sound zigzagged through air like a buzz saw. She needed a buzz saw. Could she operate one without mangling her own flesh?

Gary or Larry pulled her toward him. His uncircumcised penis spilled out of his purple — Jesus, purple? — briefs and faced her like a big, bouncing Shar-Pei puppy. Did Dumb-ass have a blue-black tongue, too?

She laughed, mostly twitches and snorts. Shar-Pei started folding in on its wrinkly self.

Dumb-ass slapped her. Hard. Her cheek felt hot, scarlet as the crimson on his shirt.

While he looked down at his crotch, she thrust open the passenger-side door. Fled like a cat, a dog, a deer. Through and out of the park.

DOGS

Deep-fried. Ambrosial coating. She shuts her eyes, concentrating on the crunch in her thirteen-year-old mouth. Then a dark presence. Three dark presences. Eyes open. Three tall dirty-blond dudes, with thick beet-red necks, staring. Perspiration beads her forehead. She can no longer differentiate wiener from batter, lecher from loser. Walks away.

EXCUSES

Didn't write home from camp — lost my pencil. Father called, said: "Demand another!"

Growing up, avoided dish washing, laundry hanging, any type of vacuuming. Opted for drawing, writing, singing. (But did chores, too; no choice.)

Never learned to brew coffee. Preferred not to prepare it. For anyone.

Chose not to request a raise. (None merited; hadn't improved.)

Piled on pounds for years. Noodles substituted for hope.

Waited so long to break up with a former boyfriend — though he was cheap as sequins and fun chiefly in bed — that he finally dumped me.

* * * SHRED AFTER READING * * *

SAFETY FIRST

Two nights ago I dreamed my ex-husband tried to kill himself. In my dream, just home from work, I heard coughing, sputtering — from our bedroom. I ran, found him hanging by a belt from the ceiling fan. He was gasping, red-faced, kicking his legs over a knocked-over chair.

I lobbed my handbag onto the bed, rushed to the kitchen to grab a knife. Raced back. His face was nearly blue. I screamed, I cursed. I uprighted the chair and was up on it. My ex seemed to be gesturing to me with his eyes. Was he hurrying me to save him or begging me not to?

Didn't matter. I slashed through the black leather belt. Heard the thud as he crash-landed below.

In the dream he was tiny. And I was bigger, able to half-carry, half-drag him onto our bed. I left to get him a glass of water. I came back to a pink face, no sputter.

I yelled: "What the fuck is your problem?"

He began to cry, said he was sorry; he hadn't been able to see another way.

We argued. About him needing to return to therapy but not wanting to go. About me being angry all the time; him being sad, bored, and lately asexual; me being fat. The usual. With no answers in sight.

Last night I dreamed we were on our bed, my ex staring into space, me reading Ann Beattie, when he reached down to his foot and yanked off his right big toe nail. It was hanging from his toe, and blood was bubbling up from where the nail used to be.

I shrieked but was not as distraught as I'd been in the previous dream. By the second dream, I knew I couldn't save him.

AGE

Mister Guess Your Weight cringes at *grandpa*, *pops*, and *old-timer*. When a heavy-set teen shouts: "Hey, senior moment," the gray-eyed octogenarian shouts: "Get out the livestock scale!" Whatever became of *sir*, the eighty-four-year-old carny wonders.

FRANKLIN IS IN

D ue to an urgent need to urinate, Franklin had been lower-body dancing in his seat for nearly half an hour. He had finally completed his subordinates' evaluations. A quick glance at his Tissot confirmed it was just after one in the afternoon. The staff meeting was at two. He could shun his full bladder and need to refuel no longer.

The thirty-three-year-old bachelor tugged open a desk drawer. He pushed aside several clear plastic ziplock bags within — paper receipts, mini tissue packets, diminutive hand sanitizers, other sundries — until he located the right reclosable: a plastic zippered pouch containing another plastic zippered pouch stuffed with large size, polyethylene, food-handling gloves.

Franklin exhaled with relief. Every day he restocked his gloves. Every day whenever he needed them he was trepidatious, even lightheaded, until he could eye their clear pristine pouch, finger their embossed finish.

The time on his watch was now eleven after one. Franklin opened his office door, glanced left, glanced right. The hallway was clear. He strode back to his desk, stuffed a couple of gloves into a shirt pocket before hurriedly slipping on a second set.

Stepping out of his office into the hallway, he headed straight for the men's room. Too late, he spotted Shari and Elena walking in his direction. He offered a perfunctory nod. The women smiled, but he knew the pair, once they passed him, would be covering their giggling, painted mouths with germ-befouled hands.

He recalled one dreadful day, almost a month before, when the cafeteria hordes left only two vacant seats forcing Franklin and Elena to lunch together. Elena, an attractive bubbly brunette, had recently started working at the agency. His psychotherapist had been encouraging him to socialize, so Franklin did as he had been counseled — talked about something he knew.

Elena steered clear of him after that lunch, as did Shari and countless other colleagues. He kept telling himself that it wasn't his fault that one of his fields of expertise was the sanitary conditions of New York eateries. Or that he had quoted statistics on the number of establishments cited for fresh rat droppings or live roaches in dry food areas.

He should quit therapy, he thought. Or that therapist. He had concluded long ago that socializing was overrated. And, like everything else, unsanitary.

Franklin checked his watch; it was already one fifteen.

Sufficient time to expel and refuel? Franklin clucked with irritation, cracked open the door to the men's room.

The bathroom was empty. *What luck!* He opened a stall door, locked it behind him. Then he double-layered the toilet seat and sat. Through willpower and humming, Franklin survived the odious sounds and smells of micturition and defecation. A chill journeyed through him as he heard his own body betray him — tinkle, plop, fart. He held his breath, tried not to inhale. *Would it never end?*

After exiting the stall, he discarded his tainted gloves, thoroughly scrubbed and rinsed his hands — six times — before donning fresh gloves. He was grateful for the touch-free faucets and soap dispensers, the automatic hand dryers. Finally he was out in the hall.

The time on his Tissot was one thirty-seven. He grumbled to himself: *No choice — shrink-wrapped peanut-butter crackers, additive-laden apple pies from the snack machine.* Franklin refused to ponder the evening's flax seed and bran, plus the enema he'd endure afterward.

It was ten to two when Franklin arrived at the third-floor conference room. As usual he was the first to arrive. He placed his briefcase on the conference table, selecting a seat close to the exit. He refrained from drumming his clean fingers on the table, kept his well-manicured hands atop his closed briefcase. With an eye on his watch, he waited for the other psychologists.

DIME-STORE BANDITS

Twelve-year-old Imogene bought Clark's Teaberry gum and Nestlé Raisinets, five packs each, whenever she stopped off at the Bayview Luncheonette.

She needed her gum — Imogene would have explained if she'd been asked — because her mouth became parched whenever any cute boy came into view. It was as if she had been transported to a desert. No caravans. No oases. Just one giant, pulsing sun baking, baking, baking her brain.

When Imogene demolished her milk chocolate dipped California raisins, at least she knew she had consumed calcium, iron, and fiber. If an apple a day kept the doctor away, she surmised five boxes of chocolate-covered raisins would easily keep an entire hospital at bay! And an apple pie a week most certainly would keep Imogene out of the emergency room. *Puh-leaze!* Who was she kidding?

Not Mother. Mother could always tell when her eldest daughter had eaten chocolate, even from as far as ten feet away. Mother had ESP — Extra Sucrose Perception — and could detect still-invisible pimples hatching beneath Imogene's flushed cheeks.

Imogene was not the only family member who

frequented the Bayview Luncheonette. Imogene was on her way to the local eatery for her weekly stash when she spotted her ten-year-old sister Lenore's turquoise-and-white bike unchained, laid out, like a spent lover, to the left of the luncheonette's open doors. Boy, would Mother be angry if she knew Lenore was so careless! It wasn't just that somebody could steal the bicycle; someone might damage it, tripping over it, too.

Giddily, Imogene approached the tiny luncheonette. Through its plate glass storefront, she saw Lenore, already inside, edging her way alongside the cash register. The owner must have been somewhere in the back of the store. On display in front of the register were cardboard cartons of sweet temptation: Bazooka bubble gum, black licorice and red cherry Twizzlers, Nestlé Chunky bars, York Peppermint Patties, mouthwatering varieties of Clark's gum, and more. Lenore was nabbing Chunkys and Bazookas by the handful and shoving them into a back pocket. She was so quick Imogene didn't think anyone else had noticed.

Big Sister was impressed. Maybe she'd hold off from notifying Mother of Baby Sister's improprieties. After all, Mother didn't need to know everything, did she?

Imogene ducked in the clothing shop next door, pretending to examine several Hawaiian-style dresses as she watched Lenore hop onto her bike and peddle away. Big Sister chuckled to herself, left behind muumuus and a disappointed clerk, and made a beeline for Woolworth's.

About twenty minutes later, she emerged from the five-and-dime with two spiral notebooks, a pack of fuchsia pens, and a set of three white headbands in a brown paper bag. And a cat-that-killed-the-canary smile on her face. Tucked away in one jacket pocket were two drop-dead red lipsticks and one supersultry blue eye shadow. In another a stash of loose chocolate nonpareils awaited consumption. Imogene set her smiling mouth into a straight line, kept her hands away from her pockets, and headed back home.

Acknowledgments

My thanks to the publishers and editors of the various literary magazines where some of these works originally appeared, sometimes in a slightly different format or version:

Anti-Heroin Chic	"Special"
Blink-Ink	"Dogs"
The Drabble	"The New Math"
Five:2:One	"Franklin Is In"
Foxglove Journal	"Nickled-And-Dimed"
Friday Flash Fiction	"Excuses"
Jellyfish Review	"Ever After"
The Round Up Zine	"Safety First"
Spelk	"At Liberty"

Special thanks to Meg Pokrass and the members of her flash fiction workshop for their criticism, insights, and suggestions. They provided the title for the last story in this collection, "Dime-Store Bandits."

Heartfelt gratitude to my friends Madeline Artenberg, Marilyn Jaye Lewis, and Brenda Morisse who patiently read my drafts, providing honest and invaluable feedback. And to

Liz Toledo for her constant support and encouragement.

Unending gratitude to David B. McConeghey whose ear and eye for details challenge me to form more vivid characters.

I'd also like to thank Jack Cooper and Roxanne Hoffman at Poets Wear Prada for having the chutzpah to take me on.

About the Author

Iris N. Schwartz is the author of more than sixty works of fiction. She is currently working on a novel comprised of flash chapters. Her literary fiction has been published in dozens of journals and anthologies, including *Crack the Spine*, *Gravel*, *Litro*, and *Pure Slush*. In addition, Ms. Schwartz has written erotica, most notably the story "Hedonics," anthologized in *Stirring Up a Storm: Tales of the Sensual, the Sexual, and the Erotic* (Running Press). *Awakened*, a collection of her poems with those of Madeline Artenberg, was published by Rogue Scholars Press. Ms. Schwartz's story "Dogs" was nominated by *Blink-Ink* for a Best Microfiction award in 2018. Her second collection of short stories, *Shame*, was short-listed by *North of Oxford* as a 2019 summer reading recommendation. Ms. Schwartz lives in New York City with actor David B. McConeghey.

About the Artist

Meredith Marsone is an award-winning New Zealand artist with an extensive international exhibition history. Her work is held in the public collections of The Wallace Arts Trust and Trust Waikato as well as in numerous private collections around the world. During the past two years alone, her work has been exhibited in over twenty-five group shows in the United States. She's had recent solo shows in Sydney (2016) and Los Angeles (2017). A self-portrait won the coveted Lysaght Watt Trust Overall First Prize Award in 2015. Marsone has been a finalist for New Zealand's National Contemporary Art Award, Wallace Art Awards, Molly Morpeth Canaday Award, and on three occasions for The Adam Portraiture Award. She was also a finalist for Australia's Agendo Art Award. The artist lives in Blenheim, New Zealand, with her husband, three daughters, one cat, and two chickens.

ABOUT THE TYPE

Text for this book is set in Bookman Old Style, designed by Ong Chong Wah (b. 1955) for Monotype and released in 1990. The Malaysian-born graphic and font designer studied and worked in England, mostly in advertising prior to Monotype. His credits also include the ever-popular Footlight (Monotype) and Ocean Sans (Adobe) among a total of nine type families.

Ong's Bookman Old Style is characterized by the near-vertical stress of its face, heavy type color, wide letters, and the somewhat taller lowercase characteristic of hymn and classic children's books. Ong based his digitized design on various 1960s and 1970s phototypesetting revivals of Alexander Phemister's classic Old Style Antique (circa 1858) cut for the Miller and Richard foundry in Edinburgh, Scotland, as a "modern" recasting of the Caslon typeface cut by William Caslon in the 1720s.

Despite the "Old Style" tag and look — or perhaps because of it — Ong's design continues to prevail. Title designer Victoria Vaus selected Bookman Old Style for the main title of the 1999 film *Election*, a high school comedy starring Matthew Broderick and Reese Witherspoon, directed by Alexander Payne. Later the typeface was adopted for the original Tumblr logo (2007–2013) by designer Peter Vidani — prior to Yahoo! acquisition mid-2013. Bookman Old Style was chosen here for its legibility, classic storybook styling, and general good humor.